Bitza

Rules? What Rules?

AF669788

BOOKS BY ANDREW DADDO

Bitza Series

Bitza

Rules What Rules?

(Illustrated by Stephen Michael King)

Atticus Van Tasticus Series

Atticus Van Tasticus

The Map of Half Maps

The Treasure of Treasures

(Illustrated by Stephen Michael King)

Stuff Happens Series

Ned

Picture Books

Poo Face

Fart Face

(Illustrated by Jonathan Bentley)

Bitza

Andrew Daddo

Rules? What Rules?

illustrated by Stephen Michael King

PENGUIN BOOKS

PENGUIN BOOKS

UK | USA | Canada | Ireland | Australia
India | New Zealand | South Africa | China

Penguin Random House Australia

Penguin Random House Australia is part of the Penguin Random House group of companies whose addresses can be found at global.penguinrandomhouse.com.

First published by Penguin, an imprint of
Penguin Random House Australia Pty Ltd, in 2026

Text copyright © Andrew Daddo 2026
Illustrations copyright © Stephen Michael King 2026

The moral right of the author and illustrator has been asserted.

All rights reserved. No part of this publication may be reproduced, published, performed in public or communicated to the public in any form or by any means without prior written permission from Penguin Random House Australia Pty Ltd or its authorised licensees.

Penguin Random House values and supports copyright. Copyright fuels creativity, encourages diverse voices, promotes free speech and creates a vibrant culture. Thank you for buying an authorised edition of this book and for complying with copyright laws by not reproducing, scanning or distributing any part of it in any form without permission. You are supporting writers and allowing Penguin Random House to continue to publish books for every reader. Please note that no part of this book may be used or reproduced in any manner for the purpose of training artificial intelligence technologies or systems.

Cover and internal design by Tony Palmer
© Penguin Random House Australia Pty Ltd
Typesetting by Midland Typesetters, Australia

Printed and bound in Australia by Griffin Press, an accredited
ISO AS/NZS 14001 Environmental Management Systems printer

NATIONAL LIBRARY OF AUSTRALIA
A catalogue record for this book is available from the National Library of Australia

MIX
Paper | Supporting responsible forestry
FSC www.fsc.org FSC® C018684

ISBN 978 1 76 135599 8 (Paperback)

We at Penguin Random House Australia acknowledge that Aboriginal and Torres Strait Islander peoples are the Traditional Custodians and the first storytellers of the lands on which we live and work. We honour Aboriginal and Torres Strait Islander peoples' continuous connection to Country, waters, skies and communities. We celebrate Aboriginal and Torres Strait Islander stories, traditions and living cultures; and we pay our respects to Elders past and present.

For Jas and Peg. AD

For River and Tanith. SMK

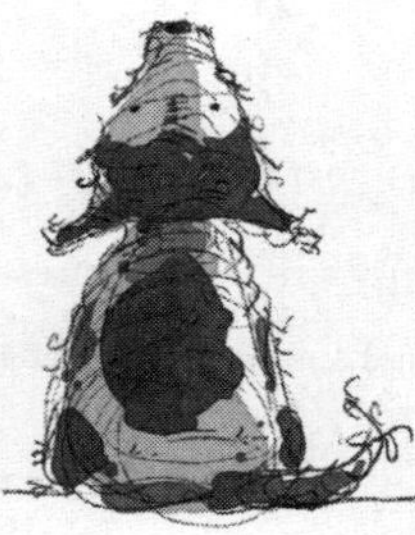

CHAPTER 1

'You're a funny dog, Bitza,' Jasper said, rolling onto her back and using me as a pillow.

The way she'd laid her head on my tummy was making me want to pee, but I didn't move because she sounded so comfy.

'I'm so glad we found each other,' she said dreamily. 'I can't believe that it was just the other day. In the park, remember? Did I find you or did you find me?'

I groaned a little, saying, '**I remember exactly. You thought I was following you home, but I was really following my ball, which was in the mouth of that other dog you**

were walking. You said I looked a bit lost and should come home with you. I was a bit lost, but now I'm not. And here we are.'

Jasper suddenly sat up. She was right in my face, an ear in each hand and rubbing away at them, making me want to lose my drool.

'Oh, Bitza, I'm so glad you found me. You're better than anything, you are. Better than ice cream. Better than fizzy drinks.

Better than an umbrella on a rainy day, or

a beach towel with no sand on it. You're the best dog in the whole wide world.'

She gave me a big squeeze. That's when I tried to wriggle away, because I really was about to burst.

'Don't you think it was fate?' Jas said, hopping off the couch and bending down to look at me. 'I wanted a dog. You needed a home. Dad was all gruff and said, *There's no way. We're not getting a dog.* But then he agreed. Remember that?' Jas sighed happily. 'He's a bit of a softy, my dad. He's your dad, too, now. It feels like we're all meant to be together. I didn't think there was much missing in our house – except for Mum – but now you're here, it feels close to properly full. You know, Bitz?'

I knew.

I knew it from the moment I followed her through my new front gate.

CHAPTER 2

I didn't even hear him come in.
I didn't hear him walk down the hall
or into the kitchen or anything.
I was too wrapped up in Jassy

talking to me. The first I knew about Dad being home was his bark.

'Is that dog on the couch?'

'No,' went Jas, throwing a pillow over me.

And you reckon Dad's a softy? I thought, trying to make myself as small as possible. *That does not sound like the bark of a softy!*

'No dogs on the couch, Jas.' This was more of a whine than a bark. He was looking at me when he did it. 'Off. OFF!' he went. He got his hands in behind me and push-pulled me off the couch.

I'd thought it was my couch. From the moment I first saw it I thought, *that looks even better than my old couch*. Maybe he meant I wasn't allowed on *that* part of the couch. Maybe this end bit was his.

I made the leap for the floor, stopping on the other side of the short table. 'Good Bitz,' he went.

I went, '**Good Dad,**' before jumping up on the other end of the couch. If that end of the couch was his, this other end must be mine.

'OFF!'

'Bitza, off the couch,' went Jas, making a lunge for me. I jumped left when she went right. I jumped right when she went left. What a game. She was hopeless at it.

'OOOOOFFFFFFF!' came a really big bark from the Top Dog.

That was enough for me, so I jumped off the couch, onto the stumpy table, sending two cups flying to the floor. I froze, as if I was invisible. Jas was to the left of me, Dad to the right. I side-eyed him first, then her. She was giggling. Dad was trying to out-side-eye me.

'Good boy, Bitz,' went Jas moving towards me.

Dad waved his finger at me and said, 'No.' He moved his finger from side to side, pointing to the ends of the couch, as if saying, *No sitting at either end of the couch.*

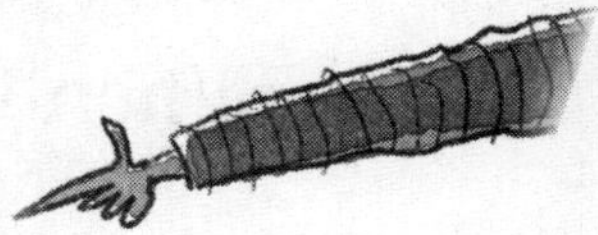

'No. No. No. No. No.'

Point. Point. Point. Point. Point.

I get it, I thought, watching him carefully. *I'm new here, this must be like a rule thing. One end of the couch is Dad's, the other belongs to Jas. Cool.*

That means, Bitza in the middle.

How good!

When I jumped back on the couch, it was right on the middle cushion. *My* middle cushion. There'd be heaps of time to creep onto their cushions later.

Dad dropped his head and shook it. His arms were folded and his whole body hurrumphed.

Jassy jumped on her end of the couch and started trying to wrestle me off.

I was like, '**It's my spot.**' So, I hunkered in harder.

She started laughing and saying, 'Get off, Bitzy. Get off!' But the more I dug in and rubbed my head against hers, the more she laughed.

Soon enough she stopped wrestling and started cuddling me.

'Before you get too comfortable,' said Dad. 'Have you taken him for a wee?'

'Oh, yeah,' Jas said, jumping up. 'Nearly forgot.'

'Take him out the front and down the road a bit,' Dad called.

‘I don’t want circles of dead grass in our backyard.’

I followed Jas in a hurry. I’d almost forgotten I was busting!

CHAPTER 3

'I know it's exciting,' Dad said quietly, maybe so I couldn't hear. 'And I know he's beautiful –'

We were all on our spots on the couch.

'He is, isn't he?'

'He really is,' said Dad.

That's when he turned to look at me. 'But there's got to be some *rules* around all of this.'

When he said 'this', he nudged his chin at me. I got it. I was 'this'. I don't think I'd ever been a 'this' before. Could a dog's day get any better?

Jas leaned across and put me in a headlock. I'm pretty sure she tried to tie my ears into a bow on top of my head, too.

Dad started talking again. 'I'm not giving up on the couch, by the way. Come springtime, he's going to start shedding hair and I don't want that all over the place. We've got to set the house rules sooner than later, okay?'

'Okay,' she said for both of us.

The way Jas rubbed my ears had me going wobbly like jelly. All I heard was 'blah blah blah couch'. I said *yes* with my eyes, even though they were closed. I wanted to say that there were heaps of couches in the house. Two inside and one outside.

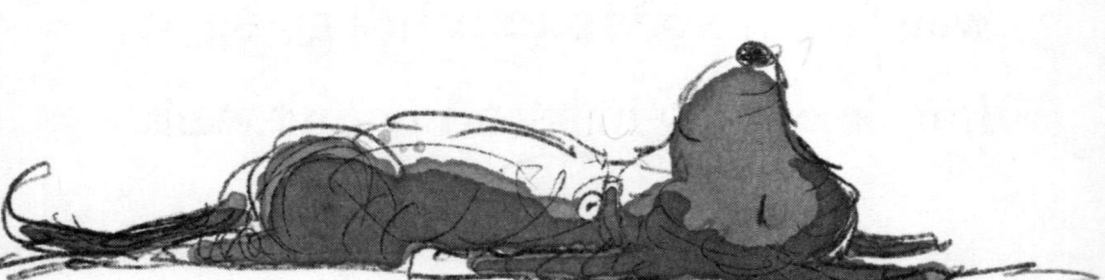

'**Aroooo. One each?**' I went, looking at Dad. It was the Blue Heeler in me, the problem-solver. One of the cool things about being one dog full of lots of breeds is I get to call on different bits of me at different times. Hound for finding things, Healer for fixing, Labrador for dinner.

'**Aroooo,**' I tried again.

'No, we're not going for a walk, Bitza,' Dad said. 'It's dark.'

'**Walk? We're going for a walk?**' I jumped down and faced him front on. '**I'll get my best ball.**'

I made it to the back door in record time, which was shut.

'**Arrooooooorrr. Come on. Open the door. I've got the perfect ball for a night-time walk.**'

'Bitza, don't scratch the door.'

Scratch. Scratch.

'Bitza!'

'**I know,**' I went. '**The stupid door. It's stuck shut.**'

Dad got to the door and flung it open before I had a chance to have another crack at it.

'Out!' he said, opening the flywire door for me. 'And don't scratch the door.'

'**Leave it open,**' was all I could manage as I headed outside.

Now, where was that ball?

CHAPTER 4

As I started sniffing around, Dad and Jas came out to the porch to watch me hunt. 'That's what I'm talking about Jassy. Stuff like that,' he said. 'He can't go scratching the door. That's a rule for him, and you have to teach him not to do that.

You have new rules, too. You've got to pick up his poop as soon as you see it, he's a big dog with big guts and you know what that means. They're like, you know. Big. Big enough to squish between your toes.'

It sounded like he was impressed, which was cool. I don't generally give the size of my back-end burnouts much thought. Maybe I should.

I stopped my hunt to watch them.

Dad had his hands on his hips and looked up at the sky.

'You know, I had a dog when I was your age. She was a beauty. Fat.

She could eat her own body weight and it didn't have to be food. She'd eat anything with a smell to it. Dirty socks were her favourite. Undies. Anything on the kitchen floor. She was a monster,' he said, smiling. 'The worst time was at your Grandnan's. We were yabbying – have we caught yabbies before? You tie a cube of meat on the end of some string and toss it in the dam. It's like fishing, the string is the line, the meat is the bait. When the yabby pulls at the meat, the line

tightens and you pull the yabby up as slowly as you can so you don't scare it. Jeez it was fun.'

'Do you eat 'em?' said Jas. 'I don't think I'd eat a yabby, sounds pretty ick.'

'**I'd eat a yabby**,' I went. '**If I knew what a yabby was**.'

Dad was leaning on the top rail of the balcony at the end of the deck. Jas copied.

'Oh, yeah, they're the best.' He gave her two thumbs up. 'Anyway, someone left their string with the meat on it out of the water.

And Tess, who'd probably talked herself into thinking she was starving, ate the meat. We all yelled at her, *Noooooo, Tess. Noooooooo!* Instead of spitting it out, she took off. By the time we caught her, all that was left was the string hanging out of her mouth.'

'What? The string that was tied to the meat?' Jas said, eyes wide. 'Dad. Tell me you went to the vet.'

'Don't be ridiculous.'

'What do you mean, don't be ridiculous? Dad. Of course

you took her to the vet. If anything like that happened to Bitza, we would *definitely* go to the vet. That's a rule, Dad. It has to be a rule.'

'Um. Maybe. But that wasn't a rule back then. So . . . we pulled the string.'

'Daaaad!' Jassy wailed.

'***Arooooooooo!***' I went.

'Tess did not like that one bit. Your Grandpa said we should wait for her to poo it out, but Grandnan said it was best to get it over with. She said, *I'm not fishing through that dog's poo looking for a ball of string. NO WAY!*

'So, me and Grandpa held Tess while Grandnan pulled on the string. It took some doing but it finally popped out with a cough.

And before it'd even landed on the ground, Tess was trying to eat it again. She was such a funny dog.'

'I never knew you had a dog.'

'Oh, yeah. I've definitely told you. I'm sure I have.' He pointed to the sky. 'I've always thought that was her star. The big one – it had to be big because she was supersized. Same way Mum's star is beautiful, because well, you know . . .'

'I know, Dad. She was the most beautiful mum ever.'

'You bet she was.'

Jassy moved in close to Dad and put an arm around his waist. 'And Bitza's the most beautiful dog ever.'

I could feel the mood change. It got all wistful and nice and I had to be part of it. I went back up on the deck and flopped at their feet.

'You can't love a dog too much, Jas.' Dad sounded like he might cry.

'That's how I feel about Bitz,' she said, digging her toes into my belly. I rolled onto my back to give her full access. Dad bent down and scratched me properly with his fingers. Paradise!

'Good girl,' he said.

'*I'm a boy,*' I groaned.

'And you're a good boy,' he said to me. 'But if we're going to get along, you'll have to learn a few of the rules around this place.'

Dad stood up to his full height and looked at Jassy. 'Dogs are a bit like kids, Jas. They need rules. And boundaries. They want to do the right thing, but sometimes the wrong thing feels pretty good, too. You know? I reckon my mum trained Tessa with food. But we could teach Bitza just about anything using a ball as a reward. He loves them.'

'Ball! That's right. I was looking for my ball!'

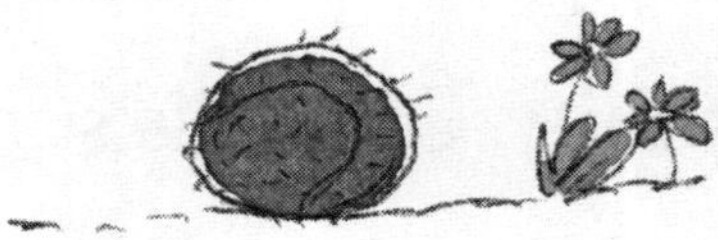

CHAPTER 5

'***Now, where's that ball?***'

I'd definitely left a ball out here somewhere. Balls have a special stink to them. Somewhere between rubber and fabric and slobber and dirt and fingers. It's hard to explain, but once you smell it you can't forget it.

It's a smell that's very, *very* hard not to love. New balls smell of opportunity. Old balls stink of history. In the pecking order of smells, balls are right up there with bones. Tennis balls are best, unless it's a rubber ball. Cricket balls are okay, like softballs or baseballs. Golf balls are a bit hard and ping pong balls are just weird.

As for bones, don't get me started with how to rank bones, it's nearly impossible.

'What's he doing, Dad?' said Jas.

I was up on the outside couch scratching between the cushions. '**Yay. A ball. Wahoo. With a bit more digging I can just . . . got it!**' I raced over to show Jas and Dad.

'**Ready,**' I went out the side of my mouth. '**Arooooooooooh!**'

'Sit, Bitza,' barked Dad. There was something in the way he said it. I dropped the ball.

'No, sit.' I picked up the ball and sat.

'Very good,' he said. There was a crinkle in the corners of his eyes.

He glanced at Jas, then gave me some side-eye. 'Drop it.'

I looked at Jas, who was trying very hard not to smile. I dropped the ball.

'Good boy,' they said together.

Dad used his foot to drag the ball towards him. 'We've been talking about the rules, Bitza –'

'Be nice, Dad. He's new. Who knows what kind of rules he had at his old house.'

Dad winked at Jas, then frowned at me. I looked at him for as long as I could, but it got pretty intense, so I looked away. When I glanced back, he was grinning at Jas. 'It's not like he really understands what I'm saying, but at least it'll be a start.'

The ball was under the arch of his foot. I could see it, and I could almost taste the way the smells of his foot and the ball were colliding. I inched closer, waiting for a chance to pounce, but he covered it all the way with his other foot.

'I know you're new here, but we have certain ways of doing things.' He sounded gruff, a bit tough.

'Yeah, Bitz. Like, no doing wees or poos inside the house.' Jas sounded nice, friendly.

'Or even in our yard. Much better in front of next door's place.' Gruff Dad, again. They were double-teaming me. Good owner, bad owner.

The smell of the two feet on the ball was unreal. '**I get it,**' I went. '**Don't wee or poop where you eat or sleep. Not much new about that.**'

'What else, Jas?' Dad looked at her hopefully.

'You're not allowed on the couch, Bitz. Not really.' She looked at Dad.

'Not when Dad's home, anyway,' she whispered.

Dad shook his head. 'Jas. No couch.'

'No couch,' she repeated, looking at me. Her head was nodding up and down. 'Noooo couch.' Up, down. Nod, nod.

On the rules went. Rules about food. Digging. Rules for walks. Rules for wees. Rules about not eating shoes. No scratching the back door rule, which grew to include scratching the flyscreen door. Even a no slobbering at the table rule.

As hard as I tried to stay awake, it was hopeless.

I tried keeping one eye open at a time, both eyes half closed, one eye half open the other closed.

I rolled onto my back and scratched a bit, looking at them upside down so gravity could hold my eyelids open, but nothing worked.

I think I might have heard a rule about not pulling on the lead. Definitely no sleeping in beds (though they didn't mention 'on' beds). When to bark, which was almost never. And even rules about scratching my itchy bits, not that I had a choice.

Jas looked to Dad with a sly smile. 'You've googled them, haven't you, Dad? Dog rules?'

'Ah, yeah, no. I haven't, actually.' He frowned. 'But, like I said, we had a dog, it's not that hard, not really. I think that about covers it, don't you?'

'It feels like there are more dog rules than human rules,' Jas said, digging her foot into my guts. It was enough to roll me over and get me paying attention.

'**Yeah,**' I went. '**Plus you've only talked about *your* rules, what about *mine*?**'

Then Dad pulled the ball out from under his feet and threw it across the yard, and I was gone.

CHAPTER 6

I was on my belly in the kitchen, fully laid out trying to cool down after chasing the ball. Dad and Jas were making some amazing food smells, which made it very hard to remember what it was I was trying to remember.

Oh, yes! '**My rules,**' I went. '**What is that smell, by the way?**'

'Olives?' said Dad. 'They're great in a pasta sauce.' He was looking like he wanted to toss one into Jas's mouth.

'Ewwwww,' went Jas.

'**First rule. No olives in pasta sauce. And while we're on food, whatever you think is enough is probably only half enough. Also, if *you* like it, there's a good chance I'll love it. No olives, though, whatever *they* are. Oh, and dinnertime is anytime, really.**

Jas was chopping something, concentrating hard. Dad was mixing. I wasn't sure if they were listening.

'Aroooo,' I went. 'I mean it. Dinnertime can be anytime. It can be now. It doesn't have to come in my bowl, either. I'm a huge believer in scraps at the table. That's why I put my head on your leg when you're eating. Trust me, it's not for a pat.'

Jas flicked a bit of cheese to the floor in front of me. 'Shhhhhh,' she whispered. 'Don't tell Dad. One of

his rules is no scabbing food in the kitchen.'

The taste was sharp. I wasn't sure I loved it, but I loved that she gave it to me.

'**And walks are a bit like dinnertime. I can do them lots of times a day. Okay? We could walk now, if you like. You could stop cooking and start walking**

and really work up an appetite then make *way* too much food and give me what's left over. Good idea?'

No one made a move for the lead.

'Hey, you two. Is anyone listening to me?'

'What's all that noise about, Bitza?' Jas licked her fingers and took to her knee in front of me. 'Is all this cooking making you hungry?'

‘You’d better feed him, Jas. Maybe we should make that another rule. The dog eats before we do, that way he won’t badger us while we eat. What do you reckon?’

He was headed outside as he said it but was back soon enough with my dog bowl.

‘That’s a good rule, Dad. I like that one.’ Jas pushed me away from the cupboard and pulled out the tub with my food in it.

‘**So *that’s* where it is,**’ I barked. ‘**I’ll have to find a way to open that cupboard.**’

Jas cracked the lid and the smell was all over the place. I wagged my tail so hard I thought it'd come off.

'Good boy, outside. Come on, Bitz. Sit.' I sat. 'Shake.'

I'm definitely shaking, I thought. *I need that food*.

'No . . . shake. Shaaaaaake.' She had her hand out, so I shook. 'Other hand?' I shook that one, too.

'Good boy, Bitz.' She put the bowl down in front of me and I tried to eat all of it at once. Maybe even the bowl. 'Steady, Bitz. Go easy, boy. That's it. That's your dinner.'

'Refer to rule number one,' I tried to say through the chewing. **'What you think is enough is only half enough. Get ready for a refill, I'll be done in a sec.'**

'He's such a guts, Dad,' Jas said, laughing as she went back to the kitchen. 'Do you think he likes our new food more than his old food?'

'Dunno.' Dad stood at the door with Jas and watched me eat. 'You know something, though? You've got a friend for life out there. A dog friend. But you'll have to keep up with your human friends, too. They're just as important as your dog friend.'

'Oh, Dad.'

'And your Dad friend.'

'Daaaaaaaad.'

I watched as she smooshed up to him and gave him the kind of cuddle I wished I was sandwiched in, but nothing got in the way of dinner.

I'd lost interest in telling them all my rules. It didn't matter.

I had a feeling they already knew my cuddle rule, which was kind of like ball throwing and food and going for walks. Any time was the best time.

There was plenty more time to teach them about leaving the car window open just enough to get my head out or let the smells in.

There was another rule, a big one, but all I could think about was having a drink to wash down dinner.

Slurp slurp. There was water all around the bowl now. A good, proper mess.

Then I remembered my BIG rule. I looked in the kitchen, but they were gone.

I found them at the table, their dinner smelling almost as good as mine. I went for the spot right between their four feet and lay down. There'd be no scraps for a while.

'There you go,' Dad said. 'He eats first then leaves us in peace while we eat.' He sounded so proud of himself.

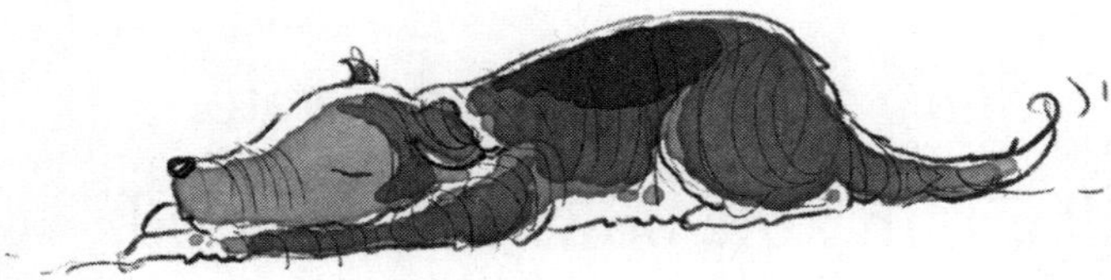

'**Rooooof,**' I went, a bit half-hearted. A big feed will do that to a dog. Then I remembered the most important thing of all, so I told them. '**Me and you and Dad,**' I went. '**We're better together.**'

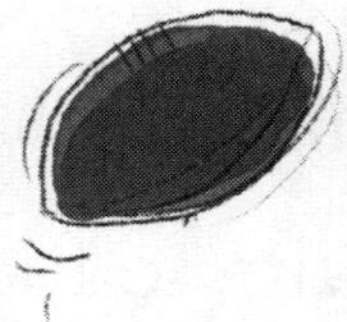

CHAPTER 7

'Alright, you two,' went the Top Dog, standing at the kitchen door. 'I'm off to work. Make sure you get out for a walk with Bitz today, Jas. Then you've got footy training in the afternoon, right? If you get yourself to training and back, I'll pick up some fish and chips on the way home.'

'Yum! What about Bitz?' Jas said. 'Can't I take him to footy? He can meet all my friends. They're going to love him!'

'I don't think so. It's not called dog-footy training, just footy training. He'll probably chase the balls and get tangled up in everyone.' Dad was using his tough voice. 'It's a good chance to catch up with your friends, too. Bitz will be fine. You're back to school next week, I'll be at work. Best if he gets used to having some home alone time.'

'I'm just trying to spend as much time with him as I can, that's all. Before I go back to school.'

'Yeah, I get it. How about you start with taking him out for a walk,' Dad said, picking up a bag and some keys. 'I'm off now, see ya.'

'See ya, Dad.'

'Make good choices, Jas.'

'You know it.' She laughed and waved. 'He always says that,' Jas said to me as she flopped onto the couch. 'He thinks he's so funny.'

I jumped up next to her, doing my best to stay on the middle cushion.

'Naughty, naughty,' she giggled.

She was nattering away to herself and I wasn't really listening. To be honest, sometimes I just liked the sound of her voice. It's a bit dreamy. And then *I* get a bit dreamy and before I know it, I'm asleep. I've no idea how long I was out for, but when I woke up there was music playing and she had hold of my hands.

'What, Bitza? You wanna dance?' She was on her knees in front of the couch, rocking my legs from one side to the other. It did not feel good.

I pulled my paws back but she had a good hold of them, so I had to get up onto my back legs and really give them a yank. Jas stood up and started wiggling. 'Yeah, that's it, Bitza. Look at us, we're dancing.'

'I call this trying to get away.'

'Yeah, Bitza, that's it. Look at you go!'

But I wasn't going anywhere. With one big, final yank, I got my paws back safely on solid ground – or couch. Where I liked them.

'Bitza the Dancer, that's you. You're a good dancer, Bitz.' The cushions puffed up as Jas sat down and she mooshed her face against mine. 'I'll miss you when I go to footy.'

You should definitely take me with you, I said with my eyes, only she wasn't looking.

'I'll get the lead,' she said, jumping up and rushing outside. 'We'll do a quick lap round the block.'

I met her at the front gate, where she buckled me up and pulled me away from a new smell I hadn't enjoyed before. It was right there at the gate. That's one of the cool things about going for walks, the smells.

You see, if I drop a smell on a lamppost, that's my lamppost, until some other dog comes along and tops my smell. That's why dogs don't do all their wee at once, we want to own as much of the neighbourhood as we can.

I left a trace on the new smell and pretty much every other stink I found on the walk. It meant the going was slow, which was okay until Jas started flapping and saying she'd be late for footy.

Of course, that was just when I needed a poo.

'**Arooroorooroorooroo!**' I said urgently, digging my paws in and trying to get myself ready, while Jas kept tugging on the lead.

'Oh . . .' she said finally, looking a bit embarrassed. 'Sorry, Bitz. Go ahead.'

While Jas found a poo bag and a bin, I did a bit of covering up. Then our walk turned into a run home. We sped through the front door,

scrambling around the corner into Jas's room. She started stuffing things into a bag. There were shoes and clothes and even a footy, which got my tail thumping.

'I won't be gone long,' she said.

How long is long? I wondered. Who really knows when anyone's coming back? They usually do. Eventually. Not always, but almost always.

I followed Jas to the kitchen where she emptied some food into my bowl before dropping it outside on the back deck, next to my water.

'Come on, Bitz, outside.' She gave me a pat. 'I'll be back after footy. I'll even share my fish and chips with you.'

With that, she shut the back door, locked it and disappeared into the house and then out the front door. I know that because I heard her yell from outside, 'Make good choices, Bitz!'

'**Arooooooooooo!**' I went, easily loud enough for her to hear me.

CHAPTER 8

Did I fall asleep in my food?

I pulled my head out of the bowl and looked around. All quiet on the backyard front. I hadn't had a chance for a proper explore of my new forever home yet.

The hound in me took charge, sniffing out the history of the place.

It was definitely rich, someone else had being dropping a lot of smells, and most of them were under the tree with the yellow fruit.

The whole place smelt fantastic – like a buffet of different wee with lots of ingredients from foods and drinks.

There was so much going on it made me want to wee and dig at the same time.

Which I did.

Well, I didn't dig where I weed – I'm not an animal. Besides, every dog knows not to dig right under trees because that's where the roots are. Better to go a bit further out. The grass was nice and soft, so that's where I got to it. And what a spot to choose. It was full of smells with a special whiff coming from down deep. Some kind of treasure, maybe? A big old bone? Maybe lots of bones? Maybe even a boneyard?

I was well into it, going pretty hard. Bum up, head down. Casting the dirt as far as I could behind me without bothering too much where it was headed.

Then I heard something.

‘**Oi!**’

Dig, dig.

‘**Oi!**’

I stopped, looked up.

There was no one in the yard, so I got back to it. Really getting good traction, each dig going deep.

‘***Oi, New Dog.***’

I stopped, which was hard, because the deeper I dug, the stronger the smell, the closer the treasure.

‘***Over here!***’

And there, sticking through a hole in the bottom of the wooden fence in the back corner of the yard, was a nose.

‘***Oi. It's me. Next Door. Freddy.***’

After taking a few steps in the nose's direction, I stopped. ‘**Is that your name? Nextdoor Freddy.**’

‘***Ah, no, it's just Freddy. And I live next door.***’

He pulled his snout out of the hole and tried to look through it. I could see the whites of his eye, but that was about it.

Oh, my goodness. I knew that eye. '**You're the ball thief,**' I barked.

'***Finders keepers,***' whinnied Nextdoor Freddy. '***Are you digging? It sounds like you're digging.***' He clearly couldn't see down into the back of the yard where I was about to make magic happen.

'**I might be digging,**' I said. It was much too soon to know whether he was a dog I could share things with. '**I might just be sniffing.**'

'***Well, whatever you're doing, you're in the wrong spot. There's nothing down there, all the action's up here near the fence.***'

Nextdoor Feddy sounded so sure of himself. How would he know what was in my backyard? And, he was wrong. There *was* something in the spot I was digging, I just hadn't found it yet. But I would. It's the Staffy in me, I have purpose when I need it.

I could hear him running up and down the other side of his fence. Stopping, jumping, probably trying to get a look into my new yard to see what I was up to.

I got back to digging. But distraction is the enemy of concentration, and good smells need full attention.

From over the fence his bark was as clear as a cat's cry.

'**What's your name?**'

I stopped again. Nextdoor Freddy was back at the hole in the fence, snout poking through as far as he could. It was dirty and wet. He had a smell to him, too. Not bad, just different.

I snuck right up to his nose and had a good sniff. He had to be some kind of terrier.

Then he must have smelt me because he quickly pulled his nose out of the hole and looked with one eye then the other.

'***You're definitely the park dog. Are you staying or visiting?***'

'Staying. Forever. It's my new forever home,' I barked.

It felt so good to howl it aloud. This really was my new home, and I loved it!

The snout was under the fence again, so Nextdoor Freddy sounded a bit muffled. '*But how? How'd you get to stay?*'

I was about to head back to the dig tree. 'It's a long story,' I offered.

'*I've got nothing but time*,' went Freddy. '*Hey. Bring your nose back in here for a sec. What's that I smell?*'

I gingerly pushed my nose towards Freddy's. He must have dug out more of the hole, because his nose was further under the fence now.

'***Is that lemon? Are you digging under the lemon tree?***'

I pulled my nose back and looked at the spot where I'd been digging. '**It's a tree with yellow balls on it. And some greeny balls as well. But the yellow balls are bigger. And they smell amazing.**'

'***Do they smell like lemons?***'

I looked back to where I'd been digging. The hole was impressive. Big. Round. And deep. The kind of hole a dog can be proud of. A hole worthy of a huge bone, even. '**I'm not sure what lemons are,**' I barked. '**Hang on.**'

I ran back to the tree and picked up one of the yellow balls and nearly hurled. It was so sour I spat it out. I had to steel myself to pick it up and drop it at the hole in the fence so that Nextdoor Freddy could smell it.

'***Yep,* definitely *a lemon. Revolting. Tell me you did not put that in your mouth.***'

'**Um, okay,**' I went. But now that I *had* put it in my mouth, I was keen to know how to get the taste *out*. It was disgusting, like an old white poo you might think is food. '**Arrrgh. It's like I've eaten ants! How do I get the taste out of my mouth?**'

Freddy was silent for a moment. Then his front foot came through the hole as if he was going to dig some more – or show me his nails, which were pretty rank.

'***Chew wood,***' was what he said. '***It's the only thing you can do. Start by munching on this fence paling***

above my paw. I'll try to dig around underneath so it's easier for you. If we can get rid of this bit of fence, I'll have a much better view of what's going on.'

'And the taste of the lemons will go?' I said hopefully, taking a crack at the fence paling.

CHAPTER 9

So that's what we did.

He dug, I chewed. The bitter taste was out of my mouth in almost no time.

We made good work of the gap in the fence. It didn't take much to loosen it even more.

He pushed when I pulled, I dug and he scratched. Soon enough, we'd moved it aside and there was a hole big enough for him to get his head through, but not his body. Yet.

Lying on his guts, with his head on my side of the fence, Nextdoor Freddy watched. He looked down the yard and spotted the mound of dirt under the lemon tree. '***Nice work, but there's nothing there.***'

I went back to the hole and had another sniff. '**There's definitely something here.**'

After a few more scrapes, I jammed my nose into the dirt and tried again. Some smells can be so hard to understand. It was earthy, of course, but there was something else.

Freddy barked hard. He pushed himself against the fence with his shoulders, making the whole thing shudder.

'***Well, when you're finished with nothing, I've got something. You see all those plants on the edge of the garden bed? The flowery ones?***'

'**Aroooooo.**' I saw them.

Freddy was pretty excited. '***They're new. I saw the big fella plant them. He's hidden something underneath.***'

He tried to force his way through the hole in the fence again. I could see the palings on each side bend

with the pressure. If he really had a crack at it, he might even get through.

I went over to the edge of the garden bed, had a smell and peed on the first bush, staking my claim. Besides, I wasn't really sure what a new plant looked like, so if this was it, at least I'd look like I knew what I was doing.

'***Oh, nice power play. That one's yours, only it's not that plant. It's the next one.***'

I peed on that, as well. Then, for good measure, I peed on the rest of them. Just a squirt. Enough to say, *Bitza was here*. Then I started digging. The ground around the first bush was nice and loose, so it didn't take long to get to the bottom of things.

'**Pull it,**' barked Freddy. '**Grab the bush and pull it!**'

I did it just like he said, and the plant came up easily.

When I looked in the hole, there was nothing there. I told Freddy and he said, '***Shake it. Shake the plant. Whatever he was hiding was in the plant. I watched him do it, I'm almost sure of it.***'

I grabbed it by the stalk and shook it, carefully at first. But, like a good scratch, once you get going with something, it's hard to stop. I gave it to that plant, shaking it so hard I thought I'd shake my head off.

Through the dirt and dust and worms and leaves I could hear Freddy spurring me on.

'***Yeah. That's it! Shake it up.***'

By the time I was done, there was pretty much nothing left of the

plant, just leaves and flowers and dirt all over the place.

I looked around at the mess with a certain sense of pride, then at Freddy. '**Are you sure there was treasure in that plant?**'

'***It could have been the next one. Now that I think about it, I'm pretty sure it wasn't that one you just destroyed. Awesome to watch, though. You ragdolled that badboy. Try the next one. Yeah. For sure that was it.***'

It wasn't.

Or the next one.

Or the one after.

Or even the little flowery bush after that.

It wasn't any of them.

I was exhausted. Digging is fun but it's hard work. And even though I'd had a really good time, I was a little disappointed there wasn't any treasure – only mess. I looked over to the hole in the fence to see if Freddy thought the treasure might be somewhere else. He wasn't there. There was just the hole.

So I did what dogs do.

I got down on my guts and put my head through. Just to see what I could see.

CHAPTER 10

Wow.

Amazing.

What a mess.

A crazy mess.

Like, the worst-kind-of-mess-any-dog-has-ever-made type mess.

Everything was dug up. There were mounds and holes. Plants lying on their sides or upside down or in ripped up bits scattered all around the yard.

There was an outside lounge, but you wouldn't sit on it. You couldn't. The cushions had been in a dogtooth blender and emptied all over the deck.

Yikes.

I pulled my head out of the hole and looked around at my own new yard.

It was a mess, too. Not a crazy mess. Not a disaster. Not the worst-kind-of-mess-a-dog-has-ever-made type mess, but still a mess.

What had I done?

I heard some grunting behind and turned to see Nextdoor Freddy wriggling his head through the hole.

'**Oh, yes,**' he barked. '**Getting there. You're definitely on the**

right track. This place'll be as good as mine in no time.'

I hadn't noticed it before, but he had the mad eyes going. One eye looking at me, one eye looking for me. Like a pug. And he was panting as if he'd been hard at it, which obviously, he had from the look of his nose.

'**I don't think the yard is meant to look like this,**' I said, looking back at the trouble I'd dug up. '**I think it's meant to look like it did before.**'

'***Better like this,***' he kind of laughed, doing the mad eyes again.

'You can roll in those holes for days and never get bored. It's practically perfect.'

I wasn't so sure. I had a bad feeling.

Just then, there was the sound of a door being unlocked. I turned to see if Jas was back, a bit scared and a bit hopeful, but I couldn't see anyone through the glass in the back door.

'***Whoopsie,***' went Freddy, just as a door swung open with a thud. With a whole new energy, he started trying to push himself through the hole to get into my yard. There was a panicked look to him, like trouble was on his tail.

'***Grab my nose. Pull me through. Quick. Help. Pull me through the hole!***'

That's when I heard it. A sound that started as a gurgle in the back of the throat but ended in a full roar. It was coming from Freddy's side of the fence.

'Frreeeeeeeeed. FRRRREEEEED. Arrrrrrrrrgggghhhhh! How many times have I told you NO DIGGING!'

Whoever was in Freddy's yard was yelling so hard they could barely get the words out.

'***Help me. Pull me through the hole!***'

Somehow he'd managed to get his feet under his chin and was doing some excavation work.

It was working. The hole was slowly getting bigger. His shoulders were almost through.

Dig. Dig. Dig.

Push. Push. Push.

The fence was wobbling.

I stood back and watched. What else could a dog do?

The calling from next door went on.

'Fred. FREEEEED! What have you done? What have you DONE?'

Dig. Dig. Dig.

Push. Push. Push.

'Fred you little . . .'

'**Nearly there, Bitza. Nearly there.**'

And he was. Freddy was pushing and grunting and shaking himself. The fence shook. He shook. The fence rocked. He rolled.

'A-HA! I see you now. There you are, you naughty little . . .'

His eyes were wider and nuttier than ever. Nextdoor Freddy was almost through the hole. He was very nearly Freddy in from Next Door.

Then, as if by magic, he started disappearing back to where he'd come from.

He made all the right movements to go forwards, only he was going backwards.

'Fred!

You.

Are.

In.

BIG.

TROUBLE!'

CHAPTER 11

I ran to the couch on my deck. The couch with the cushions that were still cushions. From next door I could hear more angry talking and a bit of barking, then a bit more talking and some sooking – that was Freddy for sure.

None of it was loud enough to make much sense, but it was pretty clear Nextdoor Freddy was in deep doo-doo. And not for the first time, I was guessing.

'Why, Freddy, whhyyyyyyyyyy? How many times do I have to tell you?'

Then nothing. Maybe some quiet grumbling and scraping of dirt or some cleaning up.

And then suddenly, 'Freddy noooo. NOOOOOO.
You went NEXT DOOR?'

That's when I saw her.

She was looking through the gap in the fence that Freddy had tried to escape through.

Then she backed off and I saw her hands on top of the fence. Then the top of her head. Then her eyes. That's as far as she got. Her eyes were doing wild circles as she looked into my new backyard.

I stayed right where I was.

'Did you do that?' she said, looking back to her side of the fence. 'Freddy, did you go in there and do that? You did, didn't you? Why?'

I heard Nextdoor Freddy bark.

It was soft and a bit whiny but clear enough to understand from where I was. '***Bitza did it. He did this, too. That new dog came over here through that hole and dug up our yard. I can't believe it either. I was only going through the hole to block it up and make sure he***

couldn't get through again to make even more mess.'

'Oh, Freddy. What am I going to do with you?' she said. 'At least you didn't get to their outdoor furniture, that would have been a disaster.' I could see her looking, but she wasn't doing much seeing, because she didn't seem to spot me.

There was a bit of a rattle and rumble near the fence and before long the hole was filled in and the fence paling back where it started. There was even some hammering and more fence shuddering so I guessed that was the end of that.

Only it wasn't.

When Jas came home she didn't walk through the back door, she burst through it. She was all smiles and happy and practically squealed when she saw me on the outside lounge. 'Oh, Bitza, you good boy! Did you miss me?'

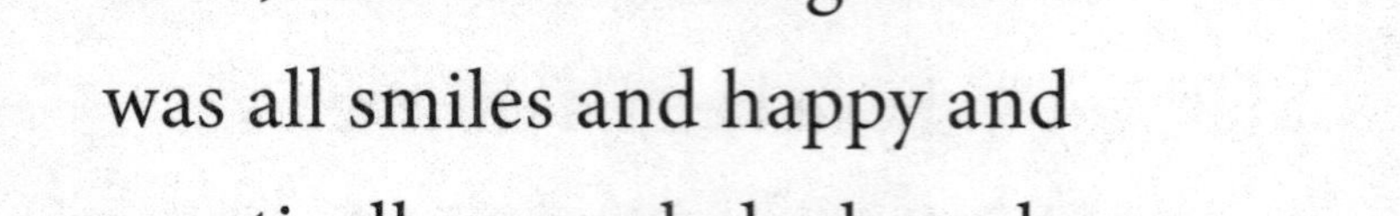

I thought I was going to wag the tail off my backside! 'Did I miss you? Did I MISS YOU?' I aroooooo'ed. 'I missed you the way a beach misses the ocean at low tide. The way a cloud misses the rain. I missed you like a Labrador misses its dinner.'

She was cuddling me and I was trying to kiss her and we laughed and giggled and then she stopped.

She went all stiff and stood up and I guessed something had happened but I couldn't think what.

Then I knew.

She'd seen it.

The garden. Or what was left of it. She took a step towards the end of the deck and I took a step towards the inside of the house. Jas took another step, and I lowered myself to the ground.

'Bitza. Did you do this?'

I got super low to the ground and was moving backwards towards the doorway. If I could get in there and onto the couch, we'd have a cuddle and a rumble and everything would be okay.

Wouldn't it?

'Bitza?'

Shouldn't it?

'Come here, Bitza. Come on.'

But I couldn't get there. It's hard to go anywhere when your legs don't want to work.

Just then, the lady from next door stuck her whole head over the fence. She looked nice. A bit nervous, but nice. 'Oh, Jasper. You're home.'

'Oh, hi, Mrs Smythe,' said Jas.

'I'm so sorry about your yard, Jas.'

Here we go, I thought. *Now I'm done for.*

Mrs Smythe went on. 'Freddy dug a hole under the fence and got in and made a terrible mess. This dog, seriously. I can come over and clean it up tomorrow, if you like. We are very, very sorry, aren't we, Freddy?' She was looking back at her own yard, and I guessed Freddy was there shaking his head.

There was a bark. It was Nextdoor Freddy. '***He did it. Jas, your new dog did this. It wasn't me. I didn't do anything.***'

'Oh, shoosh, Fred. You're a bad dog!' went Mrs Smythe from

next door. 'I really am sorry. It looks like it's just two or three plants. Much better than what the rascal's done over here.'

Jas bounced off the step and into the backyard. She grabbed two of the plants I'd ripped out and moved them near the holes they'd come from. 'It's only four plants, I can do it.' And then Jas put her foot in the crook of a tree and half climbed up so she could look over the fence into next door. 'Oh, my goodness. Freddy. What *have* you done?'

'Clearly, a lot,' said Mrs Smythe next door. 'A lot, a lot. There was a hole under the fence. I've filled it, and fixed it, so there's no way he can get through again. But, what a mess.'

'Yours is definitely worse than ours,' said Jas. And she laughed a bit, making Mrs Smythe laugh a bit as well. I thought I heard Nextdoor Freddy laugh as well, or maybe he was coughing up some dirt.

I got off the deck and walked down to Jas. It sounded as if the worst of it was over.

'Who's this?' said Mrs Smythe.

'This is Bitza, our new dog,' said Jassy, giving me a bit of a rumble around the ears. 'He's a beauty, don't you think?'

'I do.' Mrs Smythe smiled. 'What's he got? Bit of Labrador? Bit of Staffy? Bit of everything, eh?'

Jassy looked at me. 'Yep. Bits of this and bits of that.' She gave me a funny look.

'As long as he doesn't have digger in him, like our Freddy.'

Jas jumped down from the fence and rubbed at my nose. I'm almost certain some dirt came off it. 'I don't think so,' she said. 'You wouldn't do anything like this, would you, Bitza?'

The two of them talked a bit more while I took a few well needed slurps from the water bowl. As I put my head down, a sprinkle of dirt fell into it.

I shook myself tidy and looked for Jas who was on her way towards me.

She told me to sit at the back door.

I sat.

'Did you dig up our backyard?' she whispered, brushing at my ears.

I couldn't lie. But I didn't know how to tell her the truth. I just looked at her, with my head down but my eyes up. It was my way of saying, *Yes, it was me. I'm so sorry. It won't happen again (I don't think).* And I meant it.

'No digging, *especially* in Dad's garden bed,' was all Jas said. 'It's a BIG rule.' Her face softened into a smile. 'Come on, Bitz. Let's see if we can fix it up before Dad gets home.'

'Arooorooroooroooroo!'

Fallen in love with Bitza?
Need more adventures? No problem!

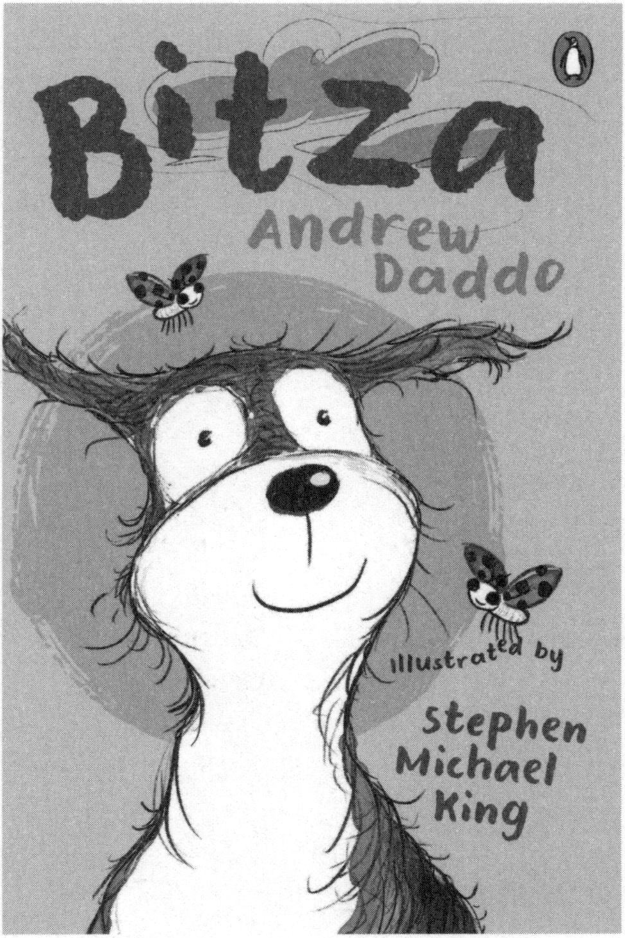

OUT NOW!

More Bitza adventures
COMING SOON!!